THE
PRINCESS
AND THE
FROG

The Junior Novelization

The movie THE PRINCESS AND THE FROG Copyright © 2009 Disney,
story inspired in part by the book THE FROG PRINCESS by E.D. Baker
Copyright © 2002, published by Bloomsbury Publishing, Inc.

Copyright © 2009 Disney Enterprises, Inc. All rights reserved. Published in the United States
by Random House Children's Books, a division of Random House, Inc., 1745 Broadway,
New York, NY 10019, and in Canada by Random House of Canada Limited, Toronto,
in conjunction with Disney Enterprises, Inc. Random House and the colophon
are registered trademarks of Random House, Inc.
ISBN: 978-0-7364-2624-4
Library of Congress Control Number: 2008941366
www.randomhouse.com/kids
Printed in the United States of America
10 9 8 7 6 5 4 3 2 1 First Edition

THE PRINCESS AND THE FROG

The Junior Novelization

Adapted by Irene Trimble

Chapter 1

The night air in New Orleans, thick and warm as red molasses, was always ready for a little magic, like a wish upon a star that might just come true. And long ago, on a summer night, one particular star was shining brightly. It was the Evening Star. Its light was just finding its way through a window to where two very special little girls sat playing on a grand four-poster bed.

The bed was covered with plump pink silk pillows. Lace curtains hung from the tall windows, and perfectly painted dolls lined the shelves. It was the room of Miss Charlotte LaBouff, one of the richest little girls in all New Orleans.

Her father, Big Daddy LaBouff, always made sure she had the best of everything.

There were many fine mansions in New Orleans, with towering white pillars and swirling vines of wrought-iron trim. They lined the streets like fancy wedding cakes in a baker's window. But the LaBouffs' house was the grandest of them all.

Charlotte and her friend, Tiana, were dressed in silk and satin. Charlotte was cuddling a soft white kitten named Marcel in her lap. Tiana and Charlotte looked like two little princesses, right down to the little crowns on their heads. Their beautiful dresses had been made by Eudora, Tiana's mother. Eudora was the finest seamstress in the city, and she often brought Tiana with her when she visited the LaBouff estate to do the final fittings. Eudora had created dozens of pretty dresses for Charlotte over the years.

Right now, Eudora was propping up a big picture-filled storybook to read aloud before she and Tiana had to leave. The two little girls were delighted. They loved it when Eudora brought out a storybook. Four-year-old Charlotte, with her blond curls and blue eyes, and five-year-old Tiana, with her dark braids and huge brown eyes, jumped off the bed and snuggled next to each other on the floor, eager to listen.

"'And just at that moment, the ugly little frog looked up with his sad round eyes and pleaded, *Oh, please, dear princess! Only a kiss from you can break this terrible spell that was inflicted on me by a wicked witch!'"*

Charlotte leaned closer to Tiana. "Here comes my favorite part," she whispered in her sweet Southern drawl. Tiana cringed as her mother turned the page—she knew what was coming next.

"'And the beautiful princess was so moved by his desperate plea,'" Eudora read, "'that she stooped down, picked up the slippery creature . . . leaned forward . . . raised him to her lips . . . and kissed that little frog!'"

Tiana closed one eye and wrinkled her nose, but Charlotte was delighted.

Eudora turned the book around to show the beautiful illustration to the two little girls. "'Then lo and behold! The frog was transformed into a handsome prince! They were married and lived happily ever after! The end!'"

"Yay! Read it again! Read it again!" Charlotte cheered, clapping her hands.

The grandfather clock in the hall had just chimed. It was already six o'clock. Eudora went to get her overcoat. "Sorry, Charlotte. It's time for us to be heading home." Turning to her daughter, Eudora gently instructed, "Say good night, Tiana."

But Tiana wasn't ready to say good night. She simply said, "There is no way in this whole wide world I would ever, *ever*—I mean *never*—kiss a frog! *Yuck!*"

Charlotte wrapped one of her long blond curls around her finger. "Is that so?" she said with a tilt of her head. She reached into her toy chest and pulled out a green frog sock puppet. She put it over her white kitten's head and grinned. Marcel squirmed.

"Well, here's your Prince Charming, Tia!" Charlotte laughed, pushing Marcel up to Tiana's nose. "Go on! Kiss him, kiss him!"

Tiana giggled and pushed Marcel away. "No! Stop it! I won't! I won't! *I won't!*"

Charlotte put her nose against Marcel's face. "I would kiss a frog," she said. "I would kiss a hundred frogs if I could marry a prince and be a princess."

Charlotte squeezed Marcel and gave him a big old kiss. The kitten squirmed harder. He twisted out of Charlotte's hands and leaped into the air, digging his claws into the ceiling in order to escape. As Marcel clung upside down from the ceiling, Charlotte picked up the sock puppet, which he had finally shaken off his head.

"You girls stop tormenting that poor little kitty!" Eudora told them as she gently pulled Marcel down and placed him on a pillow.

Just then, Charlotte's father, Big Daddy, walked into the room. Big Daddy was large and round as a barrel. He was a jolly man who always seemed to have a smile on his face.

"Good evening, Eudora!" He nodded politely.

Charlotte jumped to her feet. "Daddy! Daddy! Look at my new dress!" She twirled around for him. "Isn't it pretty?"

Big Daddy grinned at Charlotte. "Look at you!" he said proudly. Then he turned to Eudora. "Why, I'd expect nothing less from the finest seamstress in New Orleans! Marvelous work, Eudora," he exclaimed.

Charlotte showed him the pretty princess in the storybook. "Ooh, I want that dress!"

"Uh, now, sugarplum . . ." Big Daddy hesitated for a moment.

But Charlotte tugged on his mustache and begged, "I want that one! Please, please, *ple-e-e-ease!*"

Big Daddy just couldn't resist. "Eudora," he said

with a sigh, "do you suppose you could whip something up like that?"

Eudora glanced at Charlotte's closet, which was filled with princess dresses in all shapes and colors. Then she smiled and said, "Anything for my best customer."

"Yay!" Charlotte exclaimed.

Big Daddy tried his best to seem stern.

"All right now, princess, you're getting that dress, but that's it!"

Then a big grin came over his face. "Now, who wants a puppy?" Charlotte squealed with delight as Big Daddy pulled a bloodhound puppy from his pocket.

"I do! I do!" she cried out happily.

Chapter 2

Eudora took Tiana's hand and they walked out through the large wrought-iron gates of the LaBouff mansion. Gaslights flickered in the busy city as they boarded the streetcar that took them home.

Tiana sat in her usual seat next to the window and pressed her face to the glass. She watched as the elegant mansions gave way to the busy streets of downtown New Orleans, and then on to the far more modest neighborhoods.

At last the streetcar arrived at their stop. The houses there were small, but every one of them had a covered porch where neighbors would sit in the evenings, chatting and enjoying one another's company.

A warm light was shining in the window of Tiana's cozy home. She and her mother hurried in.

Tiana's father, James, had already arrived home from work and had begun making supper. He loved to cook—and he was good at it, too. His dream was to own a restaurant one day, where his food would make people's taste buds tingle with delight. He had even picked out a spot: the old sugar mill down by the river.

Right now, he was swiftly slicing some carrots to add to a steaming pot on the stove. He was making gumbo tonight, and he had promised Tiana she could help.

Tiana climbed onto a stool next to the stove. She used a long wooden spoon and stirred the pot, adding a pinch of this and a dash of that from all the ingredients her father had arranged by the stove.

"Mmm, the gumbo smells good," James said with a wink.

"I think it's done, Daddy!"

James looked into the simmering pot. "Are you sure?" he asked.

"Mmm-hmmm," Tiana answered.

"Positive?" James said.

"Yessss," Tiana told him.

James picked up a spoon to taste the gumbo.

"Wait," Tiana said, and added a few drops of hot sauce. Then she tasted the gumbo.

"Done!" she declared.

Tiana held her breath as her father dipped his spoon into the pot. Eudora looked up from her sewing and smiled.

"Hmmm," James said as he tasted the gumbo.

"What?" Tiana asked anxiously.

"Well, this is the best gumbo I've ever tasted! Eudora, our little girl's got a gift!"

"I could've told you that!" Eudora said proudly.

James gave Tiana a grin. "A gift this special has just got to be shared."

Tiana ran out the back door. "Hey, everybody!" she yelled to the neighborhood. "I made gumbo!"

"Mmmm, smells good!" a neighbor called back. He turned to his wife. "Hey, honey, grab your pecan pie."

Soon all the neighbors filled Tiana's backyard. Everyone brought a little bit of home cooking to share. Sounds of music and idle chatter drifted through the night air.

"You see, food brings folks together from all walks of life," James told Tiana. "It warms them right up and puts smiles on their faces."

Tiana nodded and helped him dish up more gumbo. She loved everything about cooking, from choosing the ingredients to adding the hot sauce, and finally sharing her creations with family and friends who would enjoy the good food and the good times.

Later that night, as Eudora and James got Tiana ready for bed, James told Tiana, "When I open my restaurant, people are going to line up from miles around just to get a taste of my food."

"*Our* food," Tiana said. She wanted to be as good a cook as her daddy!

James smiled at his little girl. "That's right. *Our* food," he said. Then he pulled out a pen and a flyer. Tiana stared wide-eyed at the picture of a glamorous, upscale supper club. Such a restaurant was sure to be filled with the lovely aromas of the best food in town. James hoped that a flyer like this would one day advertise the restaurant of his dreams. He wrote the words TIANA'S PLACE on the flyer as the restaurant's name. Tiana grinned from ear to ear.

Outside Tiana's window, the clouds parted, and starlight fell on the little girl's face.

"Oh, look!" Tiana said, scrambling across her bed toward the window. "Charlotte's fairy-tale book said if you make a wish on the Evening Star, it's sure to come true!" Her eyes widened.

Eudora smiled and lovingly moved over next to her daughter. "Then you wish upon that star, sweetheart."

"But remember, that old star can only take you part of the way," James added. "You've got to help it along with some hard work of your own, and then you can do anything you set your mind to." James paused. He was thinking about cooking, sharing food with the neighbors and his family. He wanted Tiana to remember these good times, too— and to cherish them as much as he did. "Just promise your daddy one thing: that you'll never lose sight of what's really important."

"See you in the morning, babycakes," Eudora said as she and James tucked Tiana into bed. They closed the door as they left the room.

Tiana crawled out from under her blankets and scrambled back to the window. After looking up at the Evening Star, she shut her eyes tight.

"Please, please, please!" she wished with all her might. "Help us get our restaurant."

Tiana opened her eyes and blinked in surprise.

For just a moment, she couldn't believe what she saw. There, on the windowsill, sat a small, fat, green frog. It stared back at her, opened its mouth, and let out a loud *CROAK!* Tiana screamed and ran out the door.

Chapter 3

One night fourteen years later, Tiana, now a beautiful young lady, came home from work to that very same bedroom. She was tired. She took off her apron and emptied the change from her pocket into a coffee can in her dresser drawer. The drawer was full of jars brimming with coins.

"Well, Miss Tiana," she said to herself with a sigh, "rough night for tips. But every little bit counts."

Tiana closed the dresser drawer. She sat on her bed and rested her head on the pillow. But the next thing she knew, her alarm clock rang. Tiana blinked. She couldn't believe it. It was already time to go to her second job.

Tiana opened her closet and took out a yellow uniform. As she combed her hair, she glanced at a photograph of her father on the dresser. James had passed away, and Tiana still missed him.

"Don't worry, Daddy. We'll be there soon!"

Tiana picked up the flyer James had given her years ago—the picture of the supper club with TIANA'S PLACE written on it. She looked at the image of a lady dressed in fine clothes, standing in front of the big, fancy restaurant, and fondly remembered her plans to start that restaurant with her father. She was not about to give up on that dream now. And she knew she had a lot more work to do to get there.

Quickly, Tiana finished dressing. She didn't want to be late for her job at Duke's Diner. She caught the crowded streetcar and barely heard its bells ring as it moved through town.

Tiana looked out the window. It was close to Mardi Gras, a time when New Orleans came alive with even more food, music, people, and parties than usual. The smell of delicious food was everywhere—especially the beignets. Beignets were puffy little balls of fried dough dusted with white sugar. They were a local favorite. And Tiana made the best beignets in town. Her daddy had been right. She did have a gift for cooking.

Tiana looked through a cooking magazine as the streetcar made its way downtown. One man offered her flowers, but she hardly noticed. The street was so crowded with musicians, dancers, and other performers that they nearly blocked Tiana's way as she stepped off the streetcar. It was true what they said about New Orleans during Mardi Gras: day or night, it always seemed as if there was a party going on somewhere.

But Tiana remained so focused on getting to Duke's Diner that she almost bumped right into a marching band! She needed to get to work, save her money, and buy that old sugar mill. The only thing she *did* notice was Dr. Facilier's place. She always walked a little faster when she passed his shop.

As far as Tiana knew, "Dr." Facilier had never healed anyone. His trade was in working with spells and potions. Tiana had often heard old folks say that there was plenty of magic in New Orleans . . . but not all of it was good. Dr. Facilier practiced the art of bad magic, and Tiana wanted nothing to do with it.

Tiana saw Dr. Facilier in his top hat and undertaker's coat standing outside his shop. He cast a long shadow that Tiana could almost swear moved by itself sometimes. It gave her the shivers.

Dr. Facilier had gotten the attention of a bald man in the crowd. The man gave Dr. Facilier a few coins. The doctor stretched out his long fingers and blew a pinch of powder into the man's face. Instantly, the bald man's head grew hair! The man seemed to be overwhelmed with his newborn confidence—he had a full head of hair! A pretty girl even looked his way! Then suddenly, hair grew over the man's entire face. The girl shrieked and ran away. So did the poor man when he saw his hairy reflection in a window!

Dr. Facilier, with his shadow slinking nearby, let out a chuckle, then turned his attention to the morning paper. The headline told him that Prince Naveen from the small country of Maldonia was arriving today by ship. Dr. Facilier looked at the photograph on the front page and smiled. Perhaps the day was going to be more interesting than he had expected.

Down at the docks, photographers anxiously waited as a large white ocean liner lowered its gangplank. Dozens of flashbulbs went off. Everyone wanted to get a look at the fabulously handsome young prince.

Prince Naveen surveyed the crowd. He was delighted. He had finally arrived in New Orleans—the city of jazz, jazz, and more jazz! Quickly he tossed off his crown, replaced it with a jaunty cap, and grabbed his ukulele as he rushed down the gangplank to join in the fun. Behind the prince, his short, round valet, Lawrence, stumbled along with all the prince's heavy luggage.

As Prince Naveen merged with the crowd, he was swept up into a parade of happy people dancing and singing and playing music. They danced right past Duke's Diner, where Tiana was now busy waiting on customers. Prince Naveen winked at her as he passed by. Tiana just rolled her eyes and kept working. She didn't have time for such foolishness.

But Dr. Facilier noticed the prince at the end of a line of dancers in the parade. He raised an eyebrow as he and his shadow prepared to greet the royal visitor.

Chapter 4

Inside Duke's Diner, a spatula came down on a bell with a *DING!*

"Order up!" Buford yelled over the clatter of dishes. The short-order cook was serving up eggs and grits with lightning speed, and Tiana was carrying them to customers just as fast.

"Another coffee here, dear!" a customer called out cheerily.

"Coming right up!" Tiana said.

"Hey, Tiana!" a young woman shouted, waving. Tiana turned to see a group of her friends sitting at a table nearby.

"Morning, Georgia!" Tiana chirped.

"We're all going out dancing tonight," Georgia said. "Care to join us?"

Tiana passed a plate to a customer as she told her friends, "You know I have two left feet. Besides, I'm gonna work a double shift tonight. You know," she started to say, "so—"

"So you can save for your restaurant," Georgia interrupted. "Girl, all you ever do is work!"

"Maybe next time," Tiana said, smiling as she hurried to grab the next order.

Buford looked through the pickup window. "You talking about that restaurant again?"

"Buford, your eggs are burning," she said, hoping he'd change the subject.

"You're never going to get enough money for the down payment," he said.

Tiana put a few more plates on her tray. "I'm getting close."

"How close?" Buford asked.

"Where are my flapjacks?" Tiana asked, trying to avoid Buford's question.

Buford laughed good-naturedly, but Tiana sighed. The tips came in slowly, but she knew that just as soon as she could do her own cooking in her own restaurant, her dreams would be complete.

Just then, Big Daddy LaBouff walked into the diner. "Morning, Mr. LaBouff," Tiana said, and poured him a cup of coffee. "Congratulations on being voted King of the Mardi Gras parade!"

"Thank you, Tiana!" Big Daddy replied happily.

"That caught me completely by surprise . . . for the fifth year in a row!" Tiana smiled. "How about if I celebrate with a fresh batch of—"

Tiana was already placing a big tray of beignets in front of him. Big Daddy grinned from ear to ear.

"Got a fresh batch just waiting for you," Tiana said.

"Well, keep them coming till I pass out or run out of money!" he said.

"Oh, Tia, Tia, Tia!" Charlotte LaBouff said as she burst into the diner all aflutter. "Did you hear the news? Tell her, oh, tell her, Big Daddy!"

"Oh, yeah," Big Daddy said between bites. "Prince Naveen—"

Charlotte grabbed Big Daddy's morning paper and showed the photograph to her friend. "Prince Naveen of Maldonia is coming to New Orleans! Oh! Isn't he the bee's knees?"

Charlotte closed her eyes and smiled. "Tell her what you did, Big Daddy, tell her!"

"Well," he began, "I invited—"

But Charlotte couldn't wait. "Big Daddy invited the prince to our masquerade ball tonight! Tell her what else you did, Big Daddy! Go on."

"And he's staying—" Big Daddy started to say.

But Charlotte jumped in and interrupted again: "And he's staying—"

Big Daddy put a beignet in Charlotte's mouth. "And he's staying in our house as my personal guest!" he finished as Charlotte nodded eagerly, only momentarily silenced by the beignet.

"Oh, Lottie, that's swell!" Tiana said, smiling. Charlotte still had her fairy-tale dream of marrying a prince and becoming a princess. Maybe she would do just that. "A little word of advice, though. My mama always said the quickest way to a man's heart is through his stomach." Tiana laughed.

Charlotte glanced at Big Daddy enjoying his beignet. "That's it!" Charlotte gasped, yanking the beignet out of Big Daddy's hand and examining it.

"What just happened?" Big Daddy asked, staring at his empty hand.

Charlotte threw her arms around Tiana's neck. "Oh, Tia, you-all are a bona fide genius! I'm going to need about five hundred of your man-catching beignets for my ball tonight!"

Charlotte reached into Big Daddy's pocket and pulled out a wad of cash. "Excuse me, Daddy!" she said. She handed the money to Tiana with a smile on her face. "Will this about cover it?"

She was asking for a lot. Tiana had to make dozens and dozens of her delicious beignets before this evening's ball.

But even though she was surprised by Charlotte's request, Tiana did not hesitate for a second to agree to do the work. She was thrilled. It was more money than she could earn in six months of tips—and she would be earning it without any handouts from anybody.

"This should cover it just fine, Lottie!" she said excitedly.

Charlotte squealed with joy. "Tonight my prince is finally coming, and I'm sure as heck not letting him go!"

Tiana watched as Charlotte and Big Daddy left the diner. Overwhelmed, she turned slowly as she slid the money into her pocket. Finally, she could put the down payment on her restaurant!

Dr. Facilier, who had slipped unnoticed into the diner, now lowered the edge of his newspaper and glanced at Tiana. Lurking silently at a corner table, he had overheard every single word of the conversation between Charlotte and Tiana.

With his wicked thoughts spinning, he shared a sinister smile with his shadow. An evil plan began to come together in Dr. Facilier's mind. He was going to snare a prince.

Chapter 5

As soon as she could, Tiana made an appointment to meet the real estate agents selling the old sugar mill. She remembered visiting the place with her daddy when she was little and talking about how grand a restaurant it would be.

The long-vacant building was nearly falling down now. It had been boarded up for years. But to Tiana, it was a dusty rock she knew she could polish into a sparkling diamond.

As Tiana waited outside the old building, Mr. Fenner and Mr. Fenner, two well-dressed Southern gentlemen, lifted the FOR SALE sign out of the ground and got into their car.

"We'll have all the paperwork ready to sign first thing after Mardi Gras," the first Mr. Fenner said, smiling, as they started to drive away.

"I'll do you one better," Tiana said. "Why don't I sign them tonight when I see you at the LaBouffs' masquerade ball?"

"You drive a hard bargain, Tiana!" the other Mr. Fenner shouted as they drove off.

Tiana gazed at the exterior of the old sugar mill. This was going to take a lot of work, but she couldn't have been happier.

"Table for one, please!" came a voice from behind her.

"Mama!" Tiana beamed. She could tell that Eudora was proud and had shown up to support her daughter. And most importantly, Eudora approached Tiana holding a well-seasoned cooking pot with a bow on it.

"Here's a little something to help you get started," she said to Tiana.

"Daddy's gumbo pot!" Tears welled up in Tiana's eyes as she thought about all the times she had cooked with her father. This restaurant was the dream she had shared with him, and she wished he were here.

"I know," Eudora said gently. "I miss him, too." Then, pulling herself together, she announced, "Well, hurry up and open the door!"

The two women smiled and peeked inside. It looked bad, but Tiana saw the potential. "Oh, just look at it, Mama! Doesn't it make you want to cry?"

Tiana walked over the loose floorboards. "The maître d' is going to be right where you're standing, and over here—a gourmet kitchen! And hanging from the ceiling, a big old crystal chandelier."

Eudora looked at her daughter warmly. "You are your daddy's daughter, all right. He used to go on and on about this old sugar mill, too. Babycakes, I'm sure this place is going to be just wonderful, but it's a shame you're working so hard."

"But how can I let up now when I'm so close?" Tiana asked. "I've gotta make sure all Daddy's hard work means something."

"Tiana." Eudora sighed and looked deep into her daughter's eyes. "Your daddy may not have gotten the place he always wanted, but he had something better. He had love. And that's all I want for you, sweetheart—to meet your Prince Charming and dance off into your happily-ever-after."

But Tiana didn't understand her mother's words. "Mama, I don't have time for dancing," she said as she began cleaning. She had big dreams for this restaurant, and she could see it all in front of her, beyond the rotting wood, cobwebs, and dust.

"I'm just saying," Eudora told her, patting her hand. Then she got to work helping Tiana fix up her first table.

Tiana looked at the run-down sugar mill, and for only a moment, it glittered just like the supper club in the picture James had given her. She was more determined than ever to make her dream come true—and she did not need a Prince Charming for that!

Chapter 6

The crowds on the city streets were starting to come to life as the sun set on New Orleans. Prince Naveen was dazzled by the lights and music. Lawrence tried to keep up, but the prince's heavy luggage was slowing him down, and he kept losing Naveen in the noisy bustle.

Lawrence heard a street band playing loudly in the distance. He spotted a large group gathered on a corner and pushed his way through. In the center of the crowd, Prince Naveen was playing his ukulele and dancing up a storm.

"Achidanza!" Prince Naveen exclaimed excitedly to the happy crowd.

Lawrence, sweating and exhausted, moved closer to Prince Naveen. "Sire, I've been looking for you everywhere."

"Oh, what a coincidence, Lawrence," the prince said with a chuckle in his charming Maldonian accent. "I have been avoiding you everywhere."

Lawrence was becoming more agitated. "We're going to be late for the masquerade ball," he said frantically.

Prince Naveen paid no attention. "Listen, Lawrence, listen," he said, closing his eyes and smiling. "Ah, it's jazz! It's jazz music! It was born here! It's beautiful, no?"

"No!" Lawrence told him.

As Prince Naveen continued enjoying himself and Lawrence continued not enjoying himself, Dr. Facilier watched them from behind his newspaper in a nearby alley.

"We were supposed to be at the LaBouff estate by now," Lawrence said, almost out of breath. "At this point you have two choices: woo and marry a rich young lady or get a *job!*"

Lawrence pointed to a street sweeper. Prince Naveen cringed at the very idea of work. "Ewww. All right, fine, but first we dance!"

Prince Naveen lifted Lawrence off the ground and swung him around like a rag doll.

"No," Lawrence shouted, "this is idiocy!"

"For someone who cannot see his feet, you are very light on them!" Prince Naveen laughed as he spun Lawrence in the air. Lawrence twirled around and stumbled, landing with his head lodged squarely inside a tuba.

"Perfect!" Naveen laughed. "You finally got into the music! Yes? Do you get my joke? Because your head is in a tuba."

"Get me out!" Lawrence's voice echoed from inside the instrument.

"All right, all right. Hold on," Prince Naveen said, and yanked on the short man's legs. Lawrence's head popped out of the tuba and he and the prince went sprawling to the sidewalk.

"How degrading!" Lawrence said as Naveen laughed. "I've never been so humiliated."

A dark shadow suddenly fell over Lawrence and Prince Naveen.

The prince looked up and squinted. "Uhh, hello," he said.

The tall, thin man in the top hat bowed. "Gentlemen, *enchanté!* A tip of the hat from Dr. Facilier." His voice was deep and mysterious.

Like a stage magician's trick, a business card suddenly appeared in Dr. Facilier's long fingers.

Prince Naveen stared wide-eyed at it. The card

read TAROT READINGS, CHARMS, POTIONS, DREAMS MADE REAL.

"*Achidanza!*" the prince exclaimed.

Dr. Facilier motioned for Prince Naveen to follow him down a dark alley. He smiled and glanced at Naveen's hand. "Were I a betting man, and I'm not," the smooth-talking doctor said, "I'd wager I'm in the company of visiting royalty!"

Prince Naveen was amazed. "Lawrence, Lawrence! This remarkable gentleman has just read my palm!"

"Or this morning's newspaper!" Lawrence snapped, seeing the paper with Prince Naveen's picture on the front page in Dr. Facilier's pocket. "Sire, this chap is obviously a charlatan. I suggest we move on."

Dr. Facilier shot Lawrence a withering glance, and Lawrence felt his spine turn to jelly.

Dr. Facilier waved his cane toward his shop. A glowing purple sign suddenly lit the alley. Dr. Facilier, his face long and hollow in the pale purple light, unlocked the weathered door and invited them inside.

Lawrence and Prince Naveen thought they

heard voices—ghostly voices—coming from inside the shop. But the prince eagerly stepped in. He was too excited by the wonder of it all to be cautious—and that was what worried Lawrence.

Chapter 7

Inside Dr. Facilier's dimly lit shop, Lawrence and Prince Naveen made their way past dusty shelves lined with mysterious jars that contained unidentifiable liquids and gruesome objects. Lawrence and Prince Naveen started to feel uncomfortable. The room was creepy and dark, filled with strange collections of candles, cards, and other weird items. Dr. Facilier's shadow slipped along the wall and quickly took their hats as unsettling sounds drifted through the room.

Naveen and Lawrence exchanged a nervous glance.

"Oh, that's an echo, gentlemen. It's just a little something we have here in New Orleans. A little parlor trick," Dr. Facilier said with a forboding laugh. "Don't worry."

Then, with a wave of his hand, light from an old lamp on a round table illuminated the room. Dr. Facilier sat his guests down. He showed off his potions and the bizarre masks on the wall as the ghostly voices began a quiet song.

With a snap of his fingers, a deck of cards appeared in Dr. Facilier's hand. The doctor fanned the cards enticingly and told Lawerence and Naveen to pick three each.

Naveen was delighted. They were going to have their fortunes read!

Dr. Facilier turned over Prince Naveen's first card and looked at it carefully.

Naveen was mesmerized as Dr. Facilier told him that he came from a long line of royalty. The prince nodded eagerly.

Dr. Facilier turned over the second card and shook his head sorrowfully. The card showed a royal who loved the good life but had no money.

"Mom and Dad cut you off, huh?" Dr. Facilier asked sympathetically.

Prince Naveen shrugged. "Sad but true."

Dr. Facilier leaned back in his chair and considered the problem. Then, just for a moment, the cards in the deck turned green. A twinkle lit in Dr. Facilier's dark eyes as he told Naveen that there would be lots of green in his future. The prince was thrilled at the thought of regaining his wealth.

Dr. Facilier turned over Prince Naveen's last card. It showed a prince living free from work and happy all the time. It was everything Naveen wanted!

The grinning doctor then turned to Lawrence. Dr. Facilier flipped over the valet's first two cards. Lawrence stared as Dr. Facilier told him that the cards showed he'd been bossed and pushed around all his life.

Lawrence glared at the smiling prince.

With a gleam in his eye, Dr. Facilier turned the last card for Lawrence to see. It showed a much brighter future for him—with the valet as the royal and Prince Naveen carrying his luggage. Lawrence was suddenly very excited.

Dr. Facilier stood and held out his bony hand. Lawrence jumped to his feet and shook it hard. Prince Naveen hesitated for a moment, but then Dr. Facilier flashed another smile, and the prince shook hands, as well. The deal was sealed. Dr. Facilier would bring "green" to Prince Naveen and respect to Lawrence.

"Yes!" Dr. Facilier said. The room suddenly

came alive with the sound of drums. All the masks on the walls seemed to be moving as Dr. Facilier reached his hand into one of the larger masks and pulled out a strange little talisman. Facilier's terrifying shadow danced on its own against the wall. The voices in the room were singing wildly now.

Prince Naveen sat frozen as he felt the room begin to spin. Two powerful spirit snakes wrapped around his arms and held him tight as Dr. Facilier brushed the talisman against the prince's fingertips. To Naveen's horror, the room spun faster and faster, and the ghostly voices grew louder and louder. What was happening?

Chapter 8

At the LaBouff mansion, the masquerade ball was just getting under way. The estate was aglow with colored lanterns and party balloons. Tiana, wearing a medieval costume, was busy serving beignets to the happy guests. All of New Orleans high society was there, decked out in their most lavish costumes.

Big Daddy, dressed as a Roman emperor, found his way to Tiana's serving table. He noticed that someone else had gotten to it first.

"Ah, Senator Johnson!" Big Daddy said. "I hope you're leaving some of those beignets for your constituents."

As the two men walked off, Charlotte's bloodhound, Stella, put her paws up on the table.

"Stella, no!" Tiana said, scolding the droopy-eyed dog softly. Stella whimpered. Tiana remembered the day years earlier when Big Daddy had pulled the tiny puppy out of his pocket and had given her to a surprised Charlotte.

"Okay," Tiana said, tossing the dog a beignet, "but just one."

Not far away, Charlotte anxiously paced among the partygoers. She was dressed as a fairy-tale princess, complete with a diamond crown. She was ignoring all her guests as her eyes searched the dance floor for her prince.

One young man asked her if she'd care to dance, but Charlotte told him, "Later."

"But Miss Charlotte, you said later two hours ago!" the man pleaded.

"Travis," Charlotte declared, "when a woman says *later*, she really means *not ever*. Now run along. There are plenty of young fillies dying for you to waltz them into a stupor."

Charlotte escorted Travis to the dance floor, then drifted toward Tiana's table. "Give me those napkins," she whispered. "Quick!"

"What on earth for?" Tiana asked.

Charlotte tried to discreetly blot her armpits. "I swear I'm sweating like a sinner in church!" She'd waited all evening and the prince had not arrived. "Oh, Tia, it's getting to be so late!"

"There are still a few stragglers," Tiana said.

"It's just not fair," Charlotte pouted. "My prince is never coming! I never get anything I wish for!" Charlotte tore the crown off her head and dashed up the grand staircase.

"Lottie, wait!" Tiana called to her. "Just calm down, take a deep breath."

Tiana caught up with Charlotte on the balcony. "Maybe I've just got to wish harder!" Charlotte said, choking back her tears.

She looked up at the Evening Star, closed her eyes tight, and wished as hard as she could.

"Please, please, please, please, please, please, please, please, please . . ."

"Lottie," Tiana said gently, "you can't just wish on a star and expect—"

The sound of a trumpet suddenly interrupted them. "Ladies and gentlemen," the announcer called out, "His Royal Highness, Prince Naveen!"

Charlotte and Tiana turned to see the crowd part as a tall, handsome man dressed in a striking uniform walked across the courtyard. Tiana could not believe what she was seeing. Was Charlotte's wish upon the star coming true?

As for Charlotte, it all made sense to her. She

quickly put her crown back on and fixed her makeup. She whistled for a spotlight and tossed a handful of glitter around herself.

Prince Naveen noticed her immediately. The shimmering spotlight followed Charlotte as she eagerly rushed down the grand staircase. The prince took her gloved hand when she reached the last step and, in a cloud of billowing pink silk, swept her onto the dance floor.

Tiana returned to her bignet stand and watched as they magically glided over the marble floor. She sighed.

A man dressed in a horse costume approached her. "Good evening, Tiana," he said.

Then a voice came from the back end of the horse. "Marvelous party!"

Tiana suddenly recognized the voices.

"Good evening, Mr. Fenner." She looked at the back end of the horse. "And Mr. Fenner!"

"Fine-smelling beignets," the head end said.

Tiana nodded. "They're going to be the house specialty once I sign those papers."

"Yes, about that, umm," the first Mr. Fenner started to say. His voice was hesitant.

"You were outbid," the other Mr. Fenner finished.

Tiana was shocked. "What?"

"A fellow came in offering the full amount, in cash. Unless you can top his offer by Wednesday, you can kiss that place goodbye."

Tiana was furious. "But we had an agreement. You promised!"

Mr. Fenner removed his horse head and took a beignet from her tray. "Promises are like piecrust, easily made, easily broken. Love those beignets, though." Mr. Fenner at the back end stuffed at least a dozen beignets into his costume.

The brothers began to trot away. "Wait a minute! Now, you come back here!" Tiana said, reaching out to grasp the horse's tail, trying to get the Fenners to talk to her. But the tail came off in her hand.

"No!" Tiana said as she staggered backward and fell onto her serving table. As the table collapsed, trays of beignets crashed to the ground, ruining Tiana's dress and what was left of her good mood.

Chapter 9

All atwitter, Charlotte left the dance floor. "Tia," she said, still in a daze, "time to hit Prince Charming with those man-catching beignets."

Then she noticed the broken table and poor Tiana's stained dress. "Oh, my! What happened?"

"I just . . . ," Tiana began, getting to her feet. She brushed herself off.

"Oh, hush," Charlotte said, taking her by the hand. "Come on upstairs."

As soon as the two young women entered Charlotte's bedroom, Charlotte pulled out a beautiful gown for her friend. Tiana stepped behind a screen and began to change.

Charlotte was bubbling with excitement about meeting the prince of her dreams at last. "Oh, Tia, honey, did you see the way he danced with me?" Charlotte could barely contain herself. "A marriage proposal can't be far behind. Thank you, Evening Star! You know, I was starting to think that wishing on stars was just for babies and crazy people—"

Tiana emerged from behind the screen wearing the new dress. Charlotte gasped. Tiana looked stunning—like a princess!

"Look at you!" Charlotte exclaimed. "Aren't you just as pretty as a magnolia in May?" She picked up a sparkling tiara from her vanity and placed it on Tiana's head. It was the final touch for Tiana's new princess costume. "It seems like only yesterday we were both little girls dreaming our fairy-tale dreams. And tonight they're finally coming true!"

Charlotte quickly adjusted her dress and prepared to go back to the party. She didn't notice the sad expression on Tiana's face. *Her* dream had just been crushed.

"Well, back into the fray! Wish me luck!" Charlotte chirped excitedly.

Disappointed with her own luck, Tiana picked up her soiled dress and pulled out the flyer for the restaurant before she wandered out to the balcony.

She looked up at the Evening Star. "I cannot believe I'm doing this," she said to herself as she closed her eyes and folded her hands.

"Please, please, please!" she whispered.

Sighing, she realized how ridiculous it was to wish on a star. She opened her eyes and blinked hard. A tiny frog was sitting on the railing, staring at her.

"Very funny," Tiana said, as if this were some silly joke about wishing on a star and then having a frog prince appear, ready to be turned back into a human. "So what now? I reckon you want a kiss?"

A sly look came over the frog's face. "Kissing would be nice, yes!" he said in a thick accent.

The frog had just spoken! In English! Tiana jumped and screamed. She staggered back into the bedroom, knocking over shelves of toys and storybooks.

"I'm sorry! I'm sorry. I did not mean to scare you!" the frog said, hopping into the bedroom.

Tiana grabbed a stuffed bear. "No, no, no! Wait! Hold on," the frog said as she hurled the bear at him, barely missing him. "You have a very strong arm, Princess!"

Tiana grabbed another stuffed animal, ready to attack.

"Okay, please! Put the monkey down!" the desperate little frog pleaded with her.

He hopped onto the dressing table. "Please, please, please allow me to introduce myself. I am Prince Naveen—"

Tiana grabbed a storybook. This time, she hit her mark. The book slammed down on top of the frog.

"—of Maldonia," he finished with a groan.

"Prince?" Tiana was confused. "But I didn't wish for a prince." She thought for a moment. "Hold on. If you're the prince, then who was that waltzing with Lottie on the dance floor?"

The frog shook his head. "All I know is one minute I am a prince, charming and handsome, cutting a rug, and the next thing I know, I'm tripping over these!" He lifted a green webbed foot.

Tiana held up the book, ready to slam it down again. "Wait, wait, wait!" the frog yelled, seeing the title on the cover. "I know this story!"

Tiana looked at the cover. It was that fairy tale about the girl who had kissed a frog and turned him into a prince. Tiana had loved that story—right up until the kissing part. Who would kiss a frog?

"My mother had the servants read this to me every night!" the frog said excitedly. "And this is exactly the answer! You must kiss me!"

"Excuse me?" Tiana asked the frog as he puckered his green lips.

"You will enjoy, I guarantee. All women enjoy the kiss of Prince Naveen. Come, we pucker."

The frog's throat suddenly inflated, making him look ridiculous. "That's new," he said.

Tiana shook her head. "Look. I'm sorry. I'd really like to help you, but I just do *not* kiss frogs."

"Wait a second, but on the balcony, you asked me!" the frog protested.

"Well, I didn't expect you to answer!"

"Oh, but you must kiss me," the frog pleaded. "Look, besides being unbelievably handsome, I also happen to come from a fabulously wealthy family. Surely, I could offer you some type of reward, a wish I could grant, yes?"

"Just one kiss?" Tiana said, thinking of her restaurant.

She had worked so hard to get this far. She just needed a little bit more money to open the restaurant of her dreams. It might be like a loan that she would pay back. "Okay," Tiana said to herself, "you can do this, you can do this." She leaned in and gave the frog a small kiss.

Tiana suddenly found herself swirling in a cloud of sparks and misty smoke. The last thing she heard was the pop of a magical *POOF!*

Chapter 10

When Tiana opened her eyes, all she could see was blue silk—lots of blue silk. She was somehow under a mountain of it.

"*Faldi faldonza!*" she heard the frog exclaim.

She found her way out and glanced up at the frog, who was on the dresser.

"You don't look that much different," she said. "But how'd you get way up there, and how did I get way down here?"

Tiana turned and suddenly saw herself in Charlotte's mirror. "AAIIIEEEEEE!" she screamed. Her reflection showed a frog squatting on a blue silk gown! Instead of the frog becoming a human prince, Tiana had become a frog!

"Don't panic! Don't panic!" the other frog called down to her.

"What did you do to me?" Tiana shouted. She jumped onto the dresser and struggled with Naveen. The two of them tumbled right out the bedroom window. They landed on a drum in the orchestra below. The drummer hit the cymbal, and Tiana and Naveen were catapulted into the air. They sailed over the heads of the partygoers and down the back of Charlotte's ball gown.

"Ooh!" Charlotte said with a jump as the two frogs slid down her spine. She started to squirm.

"What's gotten into that gal?" Big Daddy said as he watched Charlotte wiggle and shake around the dance floor.

Then everyone saw the two frogs.

"Hey, Stella!" Big Daddy called out to the bloodhound. "Get those frogs!"

"Run!" Naveen shrieked. He grabbed Tiana and they leaped onto the huge banquet table. Stella barreled through the crowd as they hopped across the silver trays of food.

They leaped onto Mr. Fenner and his brother, who were leaning over the punch bowl. Tiana and Naveen dove into the horse costume, climbed over one Mr. Fenner, and scrambled over the other Mr. Fenner to exit out the rear end.

"Oh, dear!" the latter Mr. Fenner cried as Stella took a bite out of the back end of his costume.

Naveen noticed the balloons decorating the lawn. He quickly grabbed a handful of balloon strings and untied them.

"Going up!" he yelled, taking Tiana's hand, and they rose into the dark sky.

From behind a statue on the LaBouff estate, Dr. Facilier glared up at the sky. Then he noticed a man running to the estate's bachelor quarters. It was Prince Naveen—the man who had just been dancing with Charlotte—except that that man was really Lawrence.

It was all part of Dr. Facilier's plan. He had turned Prince Naveen into a frog, and he had made Lawrence look exactly like the prince. But there was a problem. The talisman Lawrence wore around his neck needed Naveen for its magic to work. Without the magic, Lawrence would look like Lawrence again.

Lawrence rushed through the door and threw open a cabinet. He stared at an empty jar on the shelf and muttered, "Oh, dear."

Suddenly, the shadow of Dr. Facilier loomed silently and ominously over him.

"Oh, you're so quiet!" the startled "prince" said, turning to look at the sinister doctor.

Dr. Facilier glared at the empty jar in a rage. Naveen the frog had escaped! "You let him go!" Dr. Facilier sneered accusingly.

"The poor devil was gasping," the prince look-alike answered in Lawrence's timid voice, "so I loosened the lid ever so slightly."

Dr. Facilier backed Lawrence into a corner as his shadow moved behind him menacingly—and then tripped him.

"I—I can't go through with this!" Lawrence said, stumbling over his words. He pulled off the talisman hanging around his neck, and in an instant, he looked like his true self again. "*You* wear this ghastly thing!" Lawrence demanded as he threw the talisman. Dr. Facilier dove to catch the precious charm before it hit the floor.

"Oh, that's a grand idea, Larry. Why don't I just perform some voodoo on myself or maybe wave a magic wand and conjure up a big old pile of money?" Dr. Facilier demanded, glaring at Lawrence.

"Fun fact about voodoo, Larry: I can't conjure a thing for myself. Besides, you and I both know the real power in this world isn't magic. It's money."

Dr. Facilier held up the talisman and explained that he needed Naveen to power its magic. He replaced the talisman around Lawrence's neck, and Lawrence transformed again into the image of the real Prince Naveen.

Dr. Facilier smiled. "You just charm Daddy's little honey, win her scented hand, and we'll split the big fat LaBouff fortune right down the middle, sixty-forty, just like I said."

"But what about the prince?" Lawrence asked.

"An annoying complication we're going to sail right past," Dr. Facilier said darkly.

Chapter 11

As the two frogs floated over the dense Louisiana bayou, Tiana asked Naveen about Dr. Facilier. A blue mist hung in the air around them.

"He was very charismatic," Naveen replied as a slight drizzle began to fall.

Tiana shook her head. They saw lightning flash in the distance. "It serves me right for wishing on stars," she said. "The only way to get what you want in this world is through hard work."

"Hard work?" Naveen asked, surprised. "Why would a princess need to work hard?"

"Huh?" Tiana asked. "Oh, I'm not a princess," she said. "I'm a waitress."

Naveen was stunned. "A waitress? Well, no wonder the kiss did not work. You lied to me!"

"Nah-ah-ah," Tiana told him. "I never said I was a princess."

"You never said you were a lowly waitress! You— you were wearing a crown!"

Tiana rolled her eyes. "It was a costume party, you spoiled little rich boy!" she yelled.

"Oh, yeah?" Naveen huffed. "Well, the egg is on your face because I do not have any riches!"

"What?" Tiana cried.

Naveen shrugged his frog shoulders. "I am completely broke!"

Suddenly, they both heard the sound of balloons popping. Prince Naveen looked up. "Oh, no," he moaned as tree branches poked holes in the few remaining balloons he was holding. The two frogs screamed.

Tiana fell facedown in the muck. Prince Naveen landed on top of her with a plop.

Tiana raised her head. Her face was covered with gunk. She struggled to her feet and coughed. But that didn't stop her from continuing to argue. "You said you were fabulously wealthy!"

"No, no, no," Naveen said, correcting her. "My *parents* are fabulously wealthy. But they cut me off for being a—" Naveen suddenly noticed a leech on his leg and shrieked, "Leech!" To the tiny frog, the bloodsucker was enormous!

Tiana flicked the leech off the horrified prince

and sighed. "You're broke? And you had the gall to call me a liar?" she demanded hotly.

Naveen was about to answer when a huge catfish jumped out of the water and snatched the leech from the air. Both frogs screamed and scrambled away from the murky swamp and onto the muddy shore. Trying to catch his breath, Naveen leaned on a branch—and continued the argument.

"It was not a lie," he said. "I fully intend—"

Suddenly, the branch began to move!

Tiana and Naveen looked up. Two beady eyes were staring down on them. They realized it wasn't a branch Naveen was leaning on. It was the leg of a heron—the biggest, hungriest bird either one had ever seen!

Tiana dove at Naveen and knocked him out of the way a split second before the bird's big beak slammed down. The heron raced after them as the two little frogs ran for their lives.

"I fully intend to be rich again, once I marry Miss Charlotte LaBouff. If she will have me!" Naveen gasped, hopping as fast as he could.

Tiana hopped alongside him. "You're a prince?"

"Obviously!" Naveen replied proudly.

Tiana sighed. "She'll have you."

The heron was about to scoop them up when Tiana and Naveen slid down a tree trunk that reached out over the water. The two soared through the air and landed on a floating log. Finally safe again, they watched in relief as the heron flew away into the blue mist of the bayou, apparently in search of another meal.

Tiana looked at Naveen and asked him, "Once you two are married, you're going to keep your promise and get me my restaurant, right?"

"Not so fast," Naveen answered. "I made that promise to a beautiful princess, not a lowly waitress." He looked around and noticed something cutting through the water. "Why are those logs moving?" he asked Tiana.

Tiana saw the V shapes. "Those aren't logs," she said, her voice quivering. They were alligators! *Hungry* alligators!

Tiana and Naveen dove into the water just as the alligators snapped at the log they were sitting on—a log that was actually another alligator! No wonder the heron had flown away from them!

Under the water, Tiana paddled toward the

roots of a hollow tree and swam inside. Jumping up inside the tree, she finally found a hole where she could look out. The alligators were still thrashing in search of frogs.

"Psst." Tiana heard a voice below her. She looked down at the bottom of the tree. "Lower the vine," Naveen whispered.

"Find your own tree," Tiana told him.

The hissing alligators noticed Naveen on the bank and began to swim toward him. "Look! Help me get out of this swamp," Naveen cried, "and once I marry Charlotte, I shall get you your restaurant!"

A vine dropped down in front of him. He climbed up to the dark hollow of the tree.

The rain came down harder and lightning flashed. And inside the tree, the two frogs waited out the storm until they both drifted off to sleep.

Chapter 12

Soon the early rays of the morning sun began to light up the sky. The glow filtered into the tree where Naveen was still fast asleep.

Tiana was outside building a tiny raft. She had one thing on her mind—to get back to New Orleans and try to set things right.

"Rise and shine, Sleeping Beauty!" she yelled loudly up into the tree. "We've got to get back to New Orleans and undo some of this mess you got us into."

Sleepily, Naveen hopped out of the tree and into the boat. Then he broke a twig off a nearby branch and constructed a makeshift ukulele.

"Music to paddle by," he said lazily to Tiana as he watched her work.

"I could use a little help," Tiana replied.

"I will play a little louder," Naveen suggested, strumming the ukulele a bit harder.

But before Tiana could get Naveen to stop

strumming and start working, she spotted an enormous alligator emerging from beneath the surface of the water.

Both frogs froze in terror. But to their surprise, this alligator was not interested in eating them. He was interested in Naveen's music.

"I know that song!" the alligator said excitedly.

The alligator, Louis, swished through the water until he found his trumpet, which he called Giselle. Closing his tooth-filled mouth, he put the instrument to his lips and began to blow, making sweet and lively music.

"Play it, brother!" Naveen shouted as he joined in on his ukulele. "Oh, yeah!"

"Ahhh!" Out of sheer joy, Louis screamed and grabbed Naveen, accidentally knocking Tiana off her little raft. "Where have you been all my life?" the alligator asked Naveen.

"Where *did* you learn to play like that?" asked Naveen.

Tiana looked at them both and climbed back onto her raft.

"Why, the bayou's the best jazz school in the world!" Louis answered. "All the greats play the riverboats. Oh, I'd give anything to be up there, jamming with the big boys."

"Why don't you?" asked Naveen.

"Oh, I tried once," Louis said sadly. "It didn't end well." Louis told the story of how he had once climbed aboard a riverboat to join a band. But as soon as the people saw that he was a real alligator—not a person dressed in an alligator suit—they chased him off the boat. Louis had never tried to play with humans again, but he continued to play out on the bayou, alone.

Tiana stepped up and dragged Naveen away. "It has been a real pleasure meeting you, Louis. And thank you kindly for not eating us, but we had best be on our way."

She led Naveen back to the raft.

"Where are you going?" Louis asked, crushed.

"Back to New Orleans to find somebody to break this spell," Tiana told him.

Louis looked around, confused. "What spell?"

Naveen rolled his big frog eyes. "Brace yourself, my scaly friend—we are not frogs. We are humans."

"Are you serious?" Louis asked.

"I am Naveen, Prince of Maldonia," Naveen

Charlotte would kiss a frog to become
a princess—but Tiana wouldn't! She wants to
own a restaurant someday.

Prince Naveen and Lawrence meet Dr. Facilier.

Naveen's deal with Dr. Facilier is not what he expected.

Charlotte can't wait to meet Prince Naveen
at the masquerade ball.

Tiana makes a wish on the Evening Star.

Tiana meets a frog who talks. It's Prince Naveen!

Tiana reluctantly agrees to kiss the frog.

Tiana screams. She has been
turned into a frog, too!

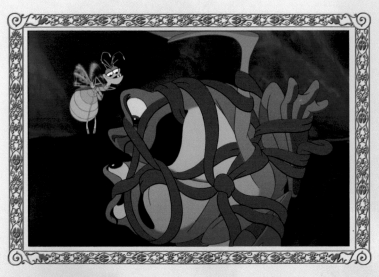

Tiana and Naveen get tongue-tied.
Ray the firefly helps untangle them.

The frogs meet a jazz-loving alligator named Louis.

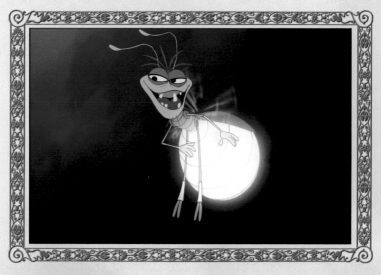

Ray is always ready to light the way.

said with a bow. "And that is Tiana, the waitress."
And then in a lower voice, he cautioned Louis, "Do
not kiss her." Louis nodded.

"Now, just a second," Tiana said to Louis. "This
goon here got himself turned into a frog by a
voodoo man, and now—"

"Voodoo?" Louis asked. "Like the kind Mama
Odie does?"

"Mama Who-die?" Naveen asked.

"Mama Odie," Louis said, incredulous that
there was anyone in the whole wide world who
didn't know who she was.

Chapter 13

"Mama Odie," Louis continued. "She's the voodoo queen of the bayou. She's got magic and spells."

"Could you take us to her?" the frogs both asked anxiously.

"To Mama Odie's? Through the deepest, darkest part of the bayou? Face trappers and hunters and cold swamp water?" Louis said, shaking his big head. "No."

Tiana sighed, disappointed. But Naveen had an idea. He leaned over to her and whispered, "Watch and learn."

He turned to the big alligator. "Louis. It is too bad we cannot help you with your dream. If only you were smaller, less toothy, you could play jazz to adoring crowds without scaring them." Naveen placed a foot on the raft and began to wave. "Anyway, enjoy your loneliness, my friend. *Achidanza!*"

"Cute," Tiana said to Naveen, "but it's not going to work."

But as Louis looked around, he suddenly saw himself sitting alone on the bank. "Hey, guys!" he yelled. "I just got a crazy idea. What if I ask Mama Odie to turn me human?"

Naveen winked at Tiana. "Louis," he called out, "you are a genius!"

"Hallelujah! I can't wait to be human!" Louis shouted. Tiana's little raft shattered as Louis hit the water. She and Naveen climbed onto him for a ride. Then the big alligator pulled out his trumpet and happily began to play a jazzy tune. Naveen joined in on his ukulele.

A group of pretty butterflies gathered around, and Naveen began to dance with them. But Tiana chased them away with a stick.

"You are getting married!" she scolded Naveen.

Naveen sighed. "Oh, right." He blew a farewell kiss to the flirtatious butterflies. "I'll just have to leave a string of broken hearts behind me!"

As the moss-covered trees closed in around them, Tiana rolled her eyes at the spoiled prince. She knew that Louis and Naveen were dreaming of being human as they played and sang. But she also knew that they only had one hope of making it happen—and it all depended on some mysterious bayou woman named Mama Odie.

At the same time that Tiana was struggling to get through the tangled swamp and endure the arrogant prince's attitude, Charlotte was at the LaBouff estate enjoying a lovely afternoon with her handsome prince.

"Oh, Prince Naveen, dear," she said as she sipped lemonade, "I am positively mortified you had to endure that frog fiasco last night."

Lawrence was sitting across from her. He was wearing the talisman, and every inch of him looked exactly like Prince Naveen.

"Well," he said suavely, "when you're next in line for the throne, you're poised like a panther, ready to expect the unexpected."

Charlotte suddenly looked horrified. "Your ear!" she shrieked, and Lawrence immediately reached up and touched it. It was as big as a cabbage—and it was bright red!

"Those pesky mosquitoes," Lawrence said, still trying to seem princely. "They are everywhere."

Lawrence was terrified that the talisman was running out of magic. He kept his hand over his ear and began speaking quickly. "Please, Miss Charlotte, I can no longer ignore the throbbing of my heart."

Lawrence's rear end suddenly expanded to twice its size! He was turning back into a fat little servant right before her very eyes.

But Charlotte was too taken by the idea that a prince was proposing to her to notice. "Land sakes, Prince Naveen!" she cried, fanning herself. "You've got me blushing."

Lawrence dropped to one knee to try to hide his expanding body as his nose grew and his teeth went crooked. He ducked low and said, "Would you do me the honor of becoming Princess of Maldonia?"

"Are you serious?" Charlotte squealed.

"As the plague!" Lawrence answered as rolls of fat began to appear under his chin.

Charlotte was thrilled. "Why, I'm all aflutter here. This is so much to absorb."

"I—I understand," Lawrence stuttered. "It's all a bit sudden."

"Yes! I most definitely will marry you!" She turned and giddily ran off. "Oh, there's so much to plan! The guest list, the dress, the music, the flowers, the shoes! We're going to have ourselves a Mardi Gras wedding!"

But just as Lawrence breathed a sigh of relief, Facilier's sinister shadow slithered over to him. "Oh, dear," the poor servant muttered. Then Dr. Facilier himself appeared and grabbed the talisman from Lawrence's neck, only to find that all its magic was gone. And with that, the last of the chubby valet's hair fell out.

"What do we do now?" cried Lawrence.

For the first time, Dr. Facilier seemed less than cadaverously cool. "I'm reduced to asking for further help from my friends from the other side," he hissed.

Lawrence gulped and glanced around nervously. He didn't know exactly who Dr. Facilier's friends were . . . and he hoped that he would never have to find out!

Chapter 14

Back in the bayou, Louis was still daydreaming about the possibilities of a magical transformation. "When we're human, I'm gonna hit the finest restaurants in the quarter! Always wanted to try red beans and rice. And then I am going to try—"

"Stop, Louis! You are making me so very hungry!" Naveen interrupted.

A small swarm of mosquitoes buzzed by the little frog's head. Automatically, Naveen's tongue snapped out, startling him. "Interesting," he said.

Tiana was disgusted. "What are you doing?"

"Shhh!" he told her quickly. "You are frightening the food!"

He snapped at another mosquito and missed. "This is harder than it looks."

Naveen's tongue snapped out again and he accidentally wrapped it around a branch. Tiana laughed as the branch cracked and Naveen fell into the water with it in his mouth.

A fly suddenly landed on a dandelion near Tiana. Her tongue instantly snapped at it. She put her hand over her mouth. "Oh, no, no, no. There is no way I'm kissing a frog *and* eating a bug on the same day!"

Her tongue darted out just as Naveen's went for the fly, too. Their tongues snared each other instead of the fly and—*SMACK!* They were suddenly nose to nose. Tiana shrieked. Their tongues were tangled together!

"Hello . . . ," Naveen said awkwardly.

Tiana tried desperately to break loose. "Hold still. Let me just see, if I go under this and over that," she managed to say with her entangled tongue.

Louis suddenly saw the frogs. "Oh, my. Hang on. Old Louis has got it covered."

He pulled and twisted them until they were in a hopeless knot.

"How's that?" Louis asked, holding the tight ball of frog tongue in his hand.

"This could be a little better," Tiana mumbled.

Louis shook his head; then his big eyes brightened. "You know what this needs?" he said, poking at the air. "A sharp stick! Be right back!"

Tiana moaned. "This is all your fault!" she said to Naveen.

"My fault, my fault? Let me tell you something! I was having a wonderful time until . . ."

The fly they had been trying to catch hovered over them and began to chuckle. He had a missing tooth and a droopy antenna. "Well, looky here. Oooh, girl, I guess you and your boyfriend got a little carried away. Am I right, am I right?" he asked, grinning.

"Oh, no, no! He is *not* my boyfriend!" Tiana said quickly.

Naveen nodded. "Do not be ridiculous. I am the Prince of Maldonia and she is a—"

"Let me shine a little light on the situation," the bug said, and wiggled a bit. A soft glow shone from his tail. "Ooooh, now that's much better, yeah!"

Tiana and Naveen were surprised. The bug was an old Cajun firefly.

He looked at the tangled frogs and sighed. "You've done this up real well, for sure." He tapped on Naveen's foot and gave him a bemused look. "Now, where does this go?" he asked himself.

He flared his light and flew down between the two helpless frogs, trying to help them.

"Hang on, Cap," he said to Naveen. "I'm just going to give a little twist here."

He held the end of Naveen's tongue and gave it a sharp yank. Tiana and Naveen unraveled and instantly sprang apart.

"It's about time I introduced myself," the firefly said to the two frogs, their tongues still hanging loose. "My name is Raymond, but everybody calls me Ray. You're new around here, huh?"

Naveen sighed. "Actually, we are from a place far, far away from this world."

"Go to bed," Ray said colorfully. "Y'all are from Shreveport?"

"Uh, no, no, no," Naveen said to the confused bug. "We are people."

Tiana explained. "Prince Charming here got himself turned into a frog by a voodoo witch doctor."

"Well, there you go!" Ray said, nodding.

"And we're on our way to Mama Odie's," Tiana continued. "We think maybe she can help."

"Whoa, whoa, whoa! Mama Odie?" Ray said.

"You-all are headed in the wrong direction, *cher*. Now, what kind of chucklehead told you to go this way?"

Louis suddenly burst from the bushes. "I found a stick!" he said, waving a branch over his head.

"Louis," Tiana said, "Ray here says you have been taking us in the wrong direction."

Louis shuffled his big feet. "Listen, I was confused by the topography, and the geography, and the choreography. Uh-huh."

Ray leaned over to Tiana and whispered, "First rule of the bayou: Never take direction from a gator."

Ray patted Tiana's arm as if to tell her there was no need to worry. Then he looked up at the night sky and whistled loudly. Suddenly, the bayou lit up with hundreds of twinkling lights. "Why, me and my relations will help show you the way," he said, smiling.

"*Achidanza!*" Naveen exclaimed.

Tiana and Naveen followed Ray as he laughed, "Keep that line flowing and the lights glowing!"

It seemed as if thousands of fireflies appeared from nowhere and lit a clear path through the bayou. They were all Ray's family and friends. It was a beautiful sight. Tiana and Naveen were amazed.

"Hey, wait for me!" Louis cried out, and dove into the water after them. Naveen and Tiana quickly hitched a ride atop the alligator. They were unable to keep their eyes off the sparkling trail of shimmering fireflies.

Chapter 15

Inside Dr. Facilier's candlelit lair, the voodoo man was busy. He turned and smiled wickedly at the masks covering his walls, calling a meeting of sorts. Dr. Facilier removed his hat respectfully.

"Friends," he said as the masks stirred. "Sorry to disturb you-all. There is this little froggy prince that lost his way, and I need your generous assistance in getting him back."

The masks stared at him with sinister looks.

"I know what you're thinking. What's in it for you?" Dr. Facilier added quickly, "Just imagine the corruption and all-around nastiness I will spread once I'm the richest man in all New Orleans. Y'all will have your evil little fingers in every nook and cranny of this fair city!"

The masks silently conferred and an agreement was reached. Soon the room was alive with menacing shadows swarming out of the masks, ready to do Dr. Facilier's bidding.

"Now we're cooking!" Dr. Facilier said, rubbing his hands together. "Search everywhere!"

Dr. Facilier struck his cane on the floor and the shadows slipped through the windows and vents of the shop. They fanned out across the rain-soaked streets of New Orleans, sliding along buildings and wrought-iron fences. A few of them even made their way toward the bayou.

A heavy mist spread over New Orleans from the LaBouff estate to the bayou, where Ray was waving goodbye to his firefly family. They had done their job, guiding Naveen, Tiana, and Louis closer to Mama Odie.

"I'll take them the rest of the way!" Ray called out. "Oh, and don't forget to tell Angela that Ray-Ray says *bonne chance!*" The little fireflies glittered off into the distance.

"Is that your girl, Ray?" Tiana asked.

"Nah," he answered. "She's my uncle's neighbor's cousin twice removed. So, you know, we're tight. But my girl is Evangeline."

Ray smiled wistfully and told Tiana, "She's the prettiest firefly that ever did glow! You know, I talk to Evangeline most every night. She's kind of shy. Don't say much, but I know in my heart that someday we are going to be together. Yeah."

Tiana smiled, too. "That's so sweet."

"Just do not settle down too quickly, my friend," Naveen said as he reclined on Louis's big tummy. "There are plenty of fireflies in the swamp."

Tiana was furious. Naveen was supposed to marry her friend Charlotte, but instead he was thinking about dating other . . . girls or frogs or whatever he was thinking. Hopping onto land, Tiana took out some of her anger at the irritating prince by hacking a trail through some bayou briar bushes. But taking to land didn't turn out as well as the companions had hoped. The much-larger Louis found it impossible to avoid the thorns.

"Ow!" he shrieked. "Pricker bushes got me! Gator down! Gator down!"

"Yeah, I can see that," Ray said as he flew over to begin pulling the painful thorns out of Louis's skin.

"EEEAAAHHH!" Louis screamed in agony.

"Hold still, you big baby!" Ray said, rolling his eyes at the alligator. "I haven't even touched it yet."

Meanwhile, Tiana and Naveen kept trying to move through the bushes.

"You know, waitress," Naveen commented, "I have finally figured out what is wrong with you."

"Have you, now?" Tiana replied.

Naveen smiled. "You do not know how to have fun. There! Somebody had to say it."

"Thank you," Tiana said, "because I figured out what your problem is, too."

"I'm too wonderful?" Naveen grinned.

"No," Tiana said firmly. "You're a lazy bump on a log!"

"Killjoy!" Naveen mumbled.

"What did you say?" asked Tiana.

"Nothing!" Naveen replied, and then hurriedly covered his next response with a pretend sneeze: "Stickinthemud!"

"Listen here, mister," Tiana lectured Naveen. "This 'stick-in-the-mud' has had to work two jobs her whole life, while you've been sucking on a silver spoon in your ivory tower!"

"Actually, it's polished marble—"

WHOOSH! Naveen's expression turned to terror as he was suddenly snatched up in a net. Tiana gasped, horrified, as she saw Naveen being carried off by a man in big rubber boots.

"Ha! Got me one, boys!" Reggie, a bayou frog hunter, yelled to his two sons. He pointed to Tiana. "Y'all get that little one over there!"

Just then, a big hand reached down for Tiana. She jumped over the gnarled hand, pulling one of the trapper's fingers back.

The hunter let out a scream. He had lost almost all his fingers trapping wild critters, and he was sensitive about the only two he had left. He reached into his belt and pulled out his throwing knives. He hurled three of them at Tiana.

Tiana felt them cut through the air and hit the tree behind her with a *whap, whap, whap!* She stared at the huge knives for a second, then hopped away as fast as she could.

Naveen was still struggling inside the net. Reggie was happy with his catch. He was thinking about a delicious meal of frog legs with a sauce picante as he climbed into his boat.

Chapter 16

Louis took one look at the hunters and dove into a nearby bush to hide. "Ahhh!" he cried. Unfortunately, he'd landed in another pricker bush.

Ray, on the other hand, realized that Naveen was in trouble!

Ray inflated his tiny chest and took off. "A bug's gotta do what a bug's gotta do," he said, flying straight up Reggie's left nostril.

Reggie yelped and let go of the net. Naveen took the opportunity to climb to the edge of the boat and dive into the water.

The boat rocked wildly as Reggie stood and jammed his finger up his right nostril. Then he blew his nose hard. Ray came shooting out and smashed into a rock.

"Oof!" Ray moaned. "I think I chipped my favorite tooth."

On the bank, Tiana was trying to get away from Two Fingers. Suddenly, his brother, Darnell, came running through the bushes waving a club.

Darnell slipped and flipped onto the muddy bank, crashing into Two Fingers. Darnell's fall tipped the log under Tiana and launched her into the air. She landed right inside Darnell's frog trap.

Darnell closed the top of the trap and whooped, "Ooh, we got one, Pa!"

"Shush, now!" Reggie said as Darnell and Two Fingers climbed into the boat.

"What happened to yours?" Darnell asked Reggie when he saw his empty net.

"Aw, shut your mouth, Darnell," Reggie said, fuming.

Naveen burst up from the swamp water gasping. He could see Tiana. She was inside Darnell's cage. And the boat was pulling away! Without a moment's hesitation, Naveen set out to rescue her. He shot his sticky frog tongue out at the boat. As the boat poured on speed, it pulled the would-be rescuer along like a water-skier.

"Pa," Darnell said, looking around, "did you just hear a suspicious thud?"

Reggie shook his head and took off his hat.

Tiana gasped. Naveen had pulled himself up to

the boat and hopped onto Reggie's head.

Darnell thought for a moment and picked up his club.

"What are y'all gawking at?" Reggie asked as Darnell suddenly swung and hit him over the head with a *BAM!*

Naveen hopped and dodged the blow.

"Ah, just missed him," Darnell said, raising the club again. He hit Reggie again but missed Naveen, who was quick on his feet.

"Two Fingers!" Reggie called out. "I need some help over here!"

Two Fingers stood up, and the frog trap's door sprang open. "Now! Go!" Naveen shouted to Tiana.

Tiana crawled out and joined Naveen. The two frogs jumped onto Two Fingers's foot.

"Watch this!" shouted Naveen, and Darnell stomped on his brother's foot with a crunch. Tiana and Naveen jumped into the air.

The two frogs hopped back and forth among the hunters until the hunters had knocked themselves silly.

At last, Darnell collapsed into a pile with Reggie and Two Fingers at the bottom of the boat.

"These two aren't like any frogs I've ever seen!" Reggie mumbled. "They're smart."

"And we talk, too!" Tiana said.

The three frog hunters, astounded by what they had heard, raced away as fast as they could. Laughing, Tiana and Naveen merrily went to find Ray and Louis.

Chapter 17

On the riverbank, Louis emerged from the pricker bush, still sore and not completely aware of what was going on. Seeing Ray on the ground, he quickly ran to help the poor firefly, who had barely escaped death inside Reggie's nose. "You all right there, little bug?" Louis asked as he used a tiny reed to fill the firefly's chest with air.

Ray choked and gasped. "I'm fine," he said, raising his head, "but your breath nearly killed me to death!"

Pointing to one of the prickly burrs in his chest, Louis asked Ray for more help. "Uh, would you mind?"

"I've got you covered," Ray said. Then he yanked the thorn from the alligator's skin.

"How about the other side?" Louis asked, turning around. Louis's entire backside was covered in prickers! This job was going to take a while.

Naveen and Tiana came strolling out of the tall

grass. They were laughing about their adventure.

"'And we talk, too!' I like it. You are secretly funny!" Naveen exclaimed.

"Not a 'stick-in-the-mud'?" Tiana asked.

"Well, I wouldn't—"

"Say it!" Tiana dared her friend. "Say it!"

"All right." Naveen took a deep breath. "You're not exactly—"

"I can't hear you," Tiana goaded Naveen. "I'm sorry. What?"

"A complete stick deep in the mud," Naveen finished, and then smiled.

Tiana giggled.

Just then, they saw poor Louis covered in painful prickers, with Ray helping him by pulling them out one at a time.

Louis babbled about how some good cooking would make him feel better.

"How about some swamp gumbo?" Tiana suggested. Naveen nodded and quickly settled in to wait as she cooked!

"Oh, no, no, no, Your Royal Highness!" Tiana scolded playfully. "You are going to mince these mushrooms!"

She handed Naveen a few wild mushrooms and a sharpened stone that he could use as a knife.

"Mince?" Naveen asked blankly.

As Tiana gathered up some ingredients from the bayou, she saw Naveen struggling to cut into the first mushroom.

He finally cut a slice and sighed, "One."

Tiana paused for a moment and looked at Naveen. She almost felt sorry for the pampered prince. "Step aside, mister," she said. "Watch and learn."

Naveen was dazzled as Tiana quickly sliced and then minced a mushroom. She handed him the knife, but he still looked confused. Tiana slid in behind him and put her hand on his. She guided the knife as they started making a pile of neatly sliced mushrooms.

Naveen was impressed. He took the knife and started slicing by himself.

"There you go!" Tiana said, smiling.

"You know," Naveen said, amazed, "I have never done anything like this before."

He sighed deeply. "When you live in a castle, everything is done for you all the time," he

88

explained. "They dress you. They feed you, drive you, brush your teeth."

"Oh, poor baby," Tiana commented.

Naveen shrugged. "Hey, I admit, it was a charmed life, until the day my parents cut me off, and suddenly I realized I don't know how to do anything."

Now Tiana began to feel genuinely sorry for him. "Well, hey," she said as Naveen kept cutting the mushroom into smaller pieces, "you have the makings of a decent mushroom mincer. Keep practicing and I just might hire you."

The praise made Naveen beam. "Really?"

"No," Tiana teased him.

"Aw, come on!" Naveen replied, laughing along with her.

As the sun set on the bayou, the shadows grew long on the glassy water. But one shadow moved with a life of its own. It had just found some broken bits of colored balloons at the bottom of a tree. The shadow let out a call that echoed through the bayou, and in an instant, other shadows joined it.

"Anyone for seconds?" Tiana asked, standing over the empty gourd she had used as a pot.

"That was magnificent!" Naveen exclaimed. "You truly have a gift!"

"Why, thank you," Tiana said, caught off guard. She was a bit surprised by the compliment coming from Naveen.

Everyone lazed happily on the riverbank after the big meal. Ray and Louis were staring dreamily into the night sky when Ray suddenly called out, "There she is, the sweetest firefly in all creation!"

"Evangeline?" Tiana asked, looking around.

Louis sat up and said, "I want to meet this girl, where is she at?"

"How can you miss her?" Ray exclaimed. "She glows right up there in front of you-all!"

They all looked up, but the only thing they could see were the stars twinkling in the sky. Then it hit them: Ray was in love with the Evening Star!

Chapter 18

Louis gazed at the Evening Star's light on the bayou. It was so beautiful that Louis felt the need to pull out his Giselle. Slowly, he began to play a tune.

Naveen extended his hand to Tiana.

"Oh, no, I don't dance," she insisted.

Naveen smiled and gave her a twirl. "If I can mince, you can dance," he said.

Tiana smiled as she and Naveen glided over lily pads and under the placid bayou water to Louis's sweet music. Tiana closed her eyes as Naveen led her in the dance. But when he leaned in for a kiss, she opened her eyes and jumped back. "Lottie is getting herself one heck of a dance partner," she said, feeling a little awkward. "We should be pushing on."

Naveen was nodding sadly when a dark shadow fell over him and began dragging him off.

"Ahhh!" Naveen screamed. "Help me!"

"Naveen!" Tiana cried as more shadows

descended on him and yanked him away.

Tiana chased after the shadows. She grabbed Naveen by the arms and tried to pull him back.

Louis appeared and joined Tiana in a tug-of-war with the evil shadows.

Ray grabbed on to Louis's tail and added his weight to the battle.

Suddenly—*FOOM! FOOM! FOOM!*—several blinding flashes of light destroyed the shadows one by one.

Tiana, Louis, and Ray looked up. An enormous, frightening silhouette was moving over a slope near a tree. They shivered in fear as the shape grew larger and larger. Then suddenly, a tiny old Creole woman appeared. She blew the smoke from the gourd she carried with her and placed her hand on her hip as she came to a stop at the base of a large tree.

They noticed that she was as wide as she was tall, about four feet in each direction. She was wearing sunglasses and had a big snake draped around her neck. They did not need to be told who this strange figure was. It was the one and only Mama Odie.

"Not bad for a hundred-and-ninety-seven-year-old blind lady!" she said to her snake, Juju. Mama Odie was proud of still being able to push a few shadows around at her age.

She waddled toward the group of friends and asked which one was in trouble with the evil Dr. Facilier.

Louis quickly pointed to Naveen. Mama Odie nodded as though the alligator was only confirming what she already knew. She turned and led them into a shrimp boat lodged in the gnarled branches of a nearby tree. She had turned the marooned boat into a house.

She put her face up to the big snake's to get a kiss. "Give us a little sugar now, Juju! You loves your mama, don't you?"

As Mama Odie settled into a chair, Tiana nervously cleared her throat and gathered her courage to speak.

Chapter 19

"Mama Odie," Tiana began, "we don't want to take up too much of your time, but—"

"Y'all want some candy?" Mama Odie asked, reaching into her pocket. She pulled out some lint, some loose change, and an old piece of candy.

"Uhh, not really," Naveen said, grimacing.

"No, no thank you," Tiana told her.

Mama Odie shrugged. "Well, now, that's too bad," she said, and popped the candy into her mouth. "It's a special candy that would have turned you human."

That caught the attention of Tiana and Naveen. Both yelled, "No! Stop!"

Mama Odie laughed. "I'm just messing with you," she said.

"How on earth did you know that we wanted to turn back—?"

Mama Odie interrupted with a snore. She had dozed off. Naveen tapped on her glasses.

"Juju!" she called out, waking suddenly. "Why didn't you tell me my gumbo was burning?"

As Mama Odie waddled over to the stove, Louis whispered, "You sure this is the right blind voodoo lady who lives in a boat in a tree on the bayou?"

"Pretty sure," Ray answered.

"I don't believe this," Mama Odie said as she stirred an old pot filled with gumbo. "I've got to do everything around here."

Tiana and Naveen hopped over to the stove. "Taste this," Mama Odie said as she shoved a spoonful of gumbo into Tiana's mouth.

"Hit it hard with a couple of shots of hot sauce, and it's the bee's knees," Tiana advised.

"Juju!" Mama Odie called out. Quick as a flash, the snake brought a bottle of hot sauce and poured it into the gumbo.

Mama Odie gave it a taste.

"Yeee-heee! That's got some zang to it! That's just what it needed," she said, smiling. Then, turning to Naveen and Tiana, she added, "Now, have you figured out what *you* need?"

"It's like what you said, Mama Odie," Tiana explained. "We need to be human."

"Ha! Y'all don't have the sense you were born with!" Mama Odie shouted. "You want to be human, but you are blind to what you need."

"What we want? What we need?" Naveen was confused. "It's all the same thing, right?"

"'It's all the same thing'!" Mama Odie exploded. "You listen to your mama now."

As Mama Odie explained the difference between *want* and *need*, Naveen seemed to understand. He had thought he wanted money. He had thought he needed to become human again to be happy. But something deep inside him began to stir as Mama Odie continued to talk. He glanced at Tiana. Then he openly stared at her. That was it— Tiana! Tiana was what he needed—and he was beginning to think that he just might want to stay with her for the rest of his life.

Unfortunately, Tiana didn't see it that way.

Mama Odie turned to her. "Do you understand what you need now, child?"

Tiana nodded. "Yes, I do, Mama Odie. I need to dig a little deeper and work even harder to get my restaurant."

"Well," Mama Odie said, throwing her hands

into the air. It didn't seem that Tiana understood anything about the difference between wanting something and needing something . . . although Naveen seemed to be starting to get it just a little bit. Sighing, Mama Odie said to Tiana, "If y'all are set on being human, there is only one way."

Mama Odie walked back to the stove and stirred the gumbo with her gourd. The thick soup started to glow. "Gumbo, gumbo in the pot. We need a princess, what ya got?"

A vision appeared in the gumbo, and Mama Odie let Tiana take a look.

"Lottie?" Tiana said, seeing Charlotte primping in front of a mirror. "But she's not a princess!"

"Hush up and look at the gumbo!" Mama Odie instructed her.

Tiana gazed back into the gumbo and saw Charlotte still sleeping. Suddenly, the door of her bedroom opened. There was Big Daddy, grinning from ear to ear. He was dressed like a king. And he was carrying a crown on a pillow. Charlotte took one look at the crown and eagerly placed it atop her head. Then she gave Big Daddy a kiss of gratitude.

"That's right," Tiana said, finally putting it all

together. "Big Daddy is King of the Mardi Gras parade, so that makes Lottie a princess."

"Does that count?" asked Naveen.

"It does till midnight, when Mardi Gras is over," Mama Odie answered. As the gumbo vision disappeared, Naveen and Tiana thought about what they had just seen: a princess who could kiss a frog—and break the spell!

Mama Odie turned to Naveen. "You've only got until then to get that princess to kiss you. Once she does—boom!—you both turn human!"

"Midnight?" Naveen repeated.

Tiana answered excitedly. "Well, that doesn't give us much time at all!"

"What about me, Mama Odie?" Louis asked. "I want to be human, too, so I can play jazz with the big boys."

Mama Odie laughed. "Jabber Jaws, dig a little deeper and you'll find everything you need." Then she addressed all four of them. "Come on, now! There's a lot of river between here and New Orleans. You best get to swimming!"

"Wait!" Louis said. "I've got a better idea."

Chapter 20

Tiana, Naveen, and Ray followed Louis into the broad, open channel of the river. They had to move fast to get to Charlotte before midnight. Finally, in the distance, they saw a stern-wheel steamboat cutting through the water. The big boat's lights glowed a soft pink as a lively jazz tune drifted through the night air.

Ray flew out and surveyed the deck. Then he whistled a signal.

Tiana and Naveen hopped off Louis and climbed up over the deck rail, looking around to make sure they would not be seen.

Louis followed. Cautiously climbing over the side, he thumped down onto the deck. Suddenly, the four friends heard some people coming around the corner. The two little frogs and Ray were able to hide, but not Louis! He was too big!

The costume-clad musicians took one look at Louis and laughed.

"Man, that is one killer-diller costume!" they shouted. "Come on and join us!" This was Louis's big chance! Barely hesitating, the alligator followed them as they went off to play jazz in a real band.

Smiling, Tiana and Ray followed, wanting to sneak a peek at Louis's big musical debut.

Meanwhile, Naveen hopped in another direction and quickly fashioned a makeshift ring. Once he finished it, he held on to what he hoped would soon be Tiana's engagement ring. Then he looked up at the Evening Star.

"Oh, Evangeline," he said. "Why can't I just look Tiana in the eye and say . . ." Naveen stopped, got down on one knee, and continued his proposal to Tiana by practicing with Evangeline. "I will do whatever it takes to make all your dreams come true. Because I love you."

Just then, Ray appeared. "Whoa, Cap! Are you making goo-goo eyes at my girl?" Ray lifted his little fists, prepared to fight for Evangeline's honor. "That's it. Put 'em up!"

"No, no! Ray!" Naveen exclaimed. "I am not in love with Evangeline! I am in love with Tiana!"

For a moment, everything stood still—even Ray.

Then the little firefly burst out, "Oooh! I knew it! I knew it! I knew it!"

"And I can no longer marry Miss Charlotte LaBouff," Naveen continued. "I will find another way to get Tiana a restaurant. I will get a job. Maybe two or three!" It seemed that the easygoing prince had had a change of heart. He was in love! And Mama Odie might say that it was exactly what he needed.

"Oh, I can't wait to tell her!" Ray exclaimed.

"No, no, no, no," Naveen said. "I must tell her! Alone."

"Oh, right!" Ray agreed.

When Naveen finally caught up with Tiana, he led her to a private corner of an upper deck. "Where are you taking me?" she asked.

"Oh, I just wanted to show you a little something to celebrate our last night together as frogs," Naveen replied.

He guided her to the top of the captain's cabin. The view was spectacular. Stars twinkled above, and lights from the buildings at the edge of the river greeted them warmly. Tiana gasped when she saw the beautiful table set with candles and food.

Naveen carefully hid the engagement ring from her. He wanted to wait for just the right moment.

"Ohhh! In all my years, no one has ever done anything like this for me!" Tiana said, pleasantly surprised.

Everything was perfect. Naveen was getting ready to present the ring when all of a sudden—

"There it is!" Tiana burst out excitedly. Unaware of what Naveen was doing, she pointed to the shore. She could see the sugar mill.

"Your restaurant?" Naveen asked with increased interest—and hope!

"Folks are going to be coming together from all walks of life," Tiana said, "just to get a taste of our food."

"*Our* food?" Naveen inquired hopefully, thinking Tiana might let him become her partner in the restaurant.

"Oh. No. My daddy." Tiana tried to explain. "We always wanted to open this restaurant. He died before it could happen. But tomorrow, with your help, our dream is finally coming true."

"Tomorrow?" Naveen asked.

"If I don't deliver that money first thing

tomorrow, I lose this place forever."

Naveen lowered the hand that held the ring. Tiana didn't see the engagement ring. All she saw was the sugar mill—and her chance to fulfill the dream that she had shared with her father. Crushed, Naveen knew that he could never come up with the money to buy the sugar mill by tomorrow. "Tiana, I love . . . the way you light up when you talk about your dream. A dream so beautiful that I promise to do whatever it takes to make it come true."

As the steamboat signaled its arrival at the docks, Naveen sadly excused himself. "I'll go round up the boys," he said, feeling as if he were saying goodbye forever.

Alone, Tiana turned to look up at the Evening Star, and spoke to her. "Evangeline," she said. "I've always been so sure of what I wanted, but now . . ." Tiana paused, as if waiting for Evangeline to reply. "What do I do? Please tell me." Tiana simply couldn't understand why, when her lifelong dream was about to come true, she felt something else tugging at her heart.

But Evangeline merely twinkled back at the

confused frog. It was as if the star knew that Tiana had to figure this out by herself.

On another part of the boat, a shadow slowly crept up behind Naveen. The shadow latched on to the frog, and nobody was nearby to rescue him. "No! Help!" Naveen yelled as a mass of shadows dragged him away.

Chapter 21

It was the biggest night of the year in New Orleans. It was Mardi Gras, and Charlotte LaBouff was dressed for the occasion. She had on the grandest wedding gown that any Mardi Gras princess had ever worn.

She rushed across the LaBouff estate and knocked excitedly on the door of the bachelor quarters. "Prince Naveen, darling. You better hurry up! Don't want to be late for our Mardi Gras wedding."

Lawrence was still his roly-poly self and fretting wildly. "Um, getting dressed!" he answered through the door. "Just a few more minutes, my dearest heart."

"Okay, honey lamb," Charlotte cooed. Turning back toward the main house, she shouted out, "Daddy, start the car!"

"Oh, my heavens! We're doomed!" Lawrence anxiously whispered to Dr. Facilier.

Suddenly, a loud rattle came from the fireplace. The air chilled as Lawrence and Dr. Facilier turned and watched a swarm of ominous shadows slipping into the room.

The shadows were dragging a green frog. It was Naveen.

"Ahhh! Much obliged, gentlemen," Dr. Facilier said to his shadow guests. He dared not offend his so-called "friends."

"Get your filthy hands off me!" Naveen yelled as Dr. Facilier grabbed him.

Then the prince recognized his valet. "Law— Lawrence!" the helpless frog exclaimed, vainly hoping for some help.

"Oh! Hold still, Your Eminence!" Lawrence said as he approached the frog, ready to use Naveen to replenish the magic in his talisman. The valet had no intention of helping the froggy prince. Naveen was on his own now.

Meanwhile, Tiana was watching Louis proudly marching off the riverboat—with a band!

Then Tiana saw Ray. "Have you seen Naveen?" she asked.

"Where's your ring?" Ray blurted out in

surprise. Then he stopped himself.

Tiana looked intently at her little firefly friend. "What are you talking about?"

Ray considered his options. Then he said cautiously, "Well, if Cap didn't say anything, I'm not going to say anything."

"Ray . . . ?"

"Okay, Cap's not going to marry Charlotte," Ray blurted out. "He's in love with you! And as soon as he gets himself kissed, he's going to find some whole other way to get you that restaurant. Uh-oh. I said too much."

"You said just enough, Ray!" Tiana exclaimed as she raced off to find Naveen. Ray followed her. They reached the torchlit parade making its way down Canal Street. Huge floats full of pirates and Arabian genies were being pulled by mules. Costumed revelers threw shiny colored beads into the cheering crowds.

"Now," Ray asked loudly, "what are we all looking for, again?"

"You just keep your eyes out for the biggest, gaudiest float with a Mardi Gras princess about to kiss herself a frog."

Ray nodded. Soon enough, a huge wedding cake float came down the street. On top was Charlotte dressed in her fabulous white gown, but next to her was no frog. Tiana froze. It was Prince Naveen—dashing, handsome, and human! And he was going to marry Charlotte! Somehow he must have already kissed her and become human, leaving Tiana to live the rest of her life as a frog.

Ray looked at poor Tiana. She was crushed. She ran from the parade, not knowing that the "prince" on the float was really Lawrence. She just saw herself staying a frog forever—and living a life without Naveen. With nowhere else to go, she sadly hopped into the city's old cemetery.

Ray flew through the wrought-iron gates and tried to comfort her. "I know what we saw with our eyes," he said, nodding, "but if we just go back there, we're going to find out your fairy tale has come true."

"Just because you wish for something doesn't make it true," Tiana said finally.

"It's like my Evangeline always says to me—"

Tiana interrupted, looking up at the sky. "Evangeline is nothing but a *star*, Ray! A big ball of hot air a million miles from here!" she yelled. "Open your eyes now, before you get hurt." She hopped away, leaving Ray alone.

Ray looked up at the Evening Star as tears welled up in his eyes. "She's just speaking out of a broken heart. That's all it is. Come on, Evangeline," he said, sticking out his tiny chin. "We're going to show her the truth!"

Chapter 22

The wedding ceremony was still going on as the royal float approached the cathedral. Dr. Facilier was enjoying the sight from a nearby balcony. He couldn't wait for the couple to say "I do."

But Naveen couldn't wait to stop them! From the little chest where he was imprisoned, he used his frog tongue to reach outside through the tiny lock. Very slowly, he stuck his tongue to the floor of the float and began inching himself and the chest closer to Lawrence's back. *SQUISH!* Lawrence stomped on poor Naveen's tongue!

The preacher asked, "Do you, Prince Naveen, take Charlotte to be your wife?"

Luckily, Ray spotted Naveen's flattened tongue and flew right over to the chest where the frog was imprisoned. "Is that you, Cap?"

"Ray!" Naveen cried. "Get me out of this box!"

Ray flexed his muscles and flew toward the prince. The problem was—could he rescue Naveen in time for the little frog to stop the wedding?

Ray flew right into the lock on the chest. He lit up and then twisted and turned while Naveen waited. Finally, after great effort, the lock sprang open! Naveen hopped out of the chest.

The wedding was almost over! Naveen jumped onto Lawrence's neck, grabbed the talisman, and held on tight.

Lawrence started jerking around.

"AAAGGGHHH!" Lawrence screamed as he stumbled backward and fell to the street below.

Charlotte was mortified. "Prince Naveen! Oh, goodness gracious! Are you all right?" she called down to him.

"I just need a moment to compose myself!" Lawrence said, getting to his feet. He was clutching the frog behind his back.

"Buttercup!" Charlotte exclaimed as she saw him duck into the cathedral. She stamped her foot. Her prince had disappeared again! "Cheese and crackers!" she fumed.

Inside the church, Naveen tried to free himself from Lawrence's grip. "Lawrence," Naveen cried, "why are you doing this?"

"As payback for all those years of humiliation!" Lawrence snapped.

None of this had escaped the notice of Dr. Facilier. He stepped out of the shadows and said to Lawrence, "Get your royal rump back on that wedding cake and finish this deal!"

Naveen shot his long tongue out and easily ripped the talisman off Lawrence's neck. Lawrence transformed back into himself—a short, squat valet.

Naveen quickly tossed the talisman to Ray. "I got it!" Ray shouted. But as the weight of the talisman pulled him down, the little firefly moaned. "It's got me, too!"

"Let go of that!" Lawrence said, stumbling toward Ray.

Dr. Facilier shook his head at Lawrence in disgust. "Stay out of sight!" he snapped.

At the same time, a horde of shadows appeared from the crowd and hurried in Ray's direction.

Ray flew right past Louis, who was playing with the riverboat band in the Mardi Gras parade. Everyone still thought he was a person in an alligator suit!

"Ray?" Louis called out. Louis could see that

Ray was no match for the shadows that were hot on his trail. The big gator tucked his trumpet under his arm and left the spotlight behind.

But Louis was too slow to keep up with his friend. He lumbered far behind the shadows, who were chasing Ray straight toward the cemetery.

Chapter 23

Tiana was alone in the cemetery when she turned and saw Ray. He threw the talisman to her. But when she grabbed the charm, the sinister shadows appeared out of nowhere and surrounded her.

Tiana raced away with Facilier's shadow close behind her. As the other shadows approached, Ray fended them off by blasting them with his light. Just then, Dr. Facilier came upon the little bug and swatted him. Ray tumbled to the ground, and the evil doctor stepped on him. The firefly was in bad shape when Louis found him.

Tiana was still running, but when Dr. Facilier caught up with her, she stopped and faced him and the deadly shadows.

"Back off, or I'll break this thing into a million pieces!" she threatened, holding the talisman high in the air.

Dr. Facilier waved his hand and blew a light powder toward her.

Something was changing. Suddenly, Tiana felt human again. She was in the restaurant of her dreams, surrounded by elegance. Her food had brought people together to share and enjoy good times, just as her father had said it would. She was a success!

The crowd in the restaurant parted, and Tiana saw Dr. Facilier. "All you've got to do to make this a reality is hand over that little old talisman of mine," the voodoo man whispered smoothly.

"No! This is not right," Tiana said nervously.

"And don't forget your poor daddy. That was one hardworking man," Facilier added.

Tiana saw a vision of her father on the back porch of their home years ago. All the neighbors were gathered around as they shared James's gumbo and chatted happily. James was loved, and he gave love to his friends and family.

Tiana finally knew exactly what to do. She had learned it from her father. "He had love!" she cried out to Dr. Facilier. "He never lost sight of what was really important. *And neither will I!*"

Tiana raised the talisman and smashed it. Instantly, everything changed. She felt herself becoming a tiny frog back in the cemetery again.

Dr. Facilier looked at the broken talisman. The darkened shadows swarmed around him viciously. Masks and dolls—just like the ones inside Dr. Facilier's lair—appeared all around. They were ready to command the shadows to take the doctor away.

"No! No! Noooo!" the doctor cried out, and in an instant, he vanished forever, leaving only his top hat behind.

Tiana took a deep breath as the shadows left the cemetery. Then she hopped down to the parade as fast as she could. She had to find Naveen.

Chapter 24

Outside the church, Charlotte was watching Lawrence being dragged away by two police officers.

Tiana hopped over just in time to hear Charlotte talking with the frog Naveen. Charlotte was only now beginning to understand that the frog was the prince—and the "prince" was Lawrence! As Princess of Mardi Gras, Charlotte merely needed to kiss the frog in front of her, and her childhood dreams would come true. The frog would be transformed back into the real, human Prince Naveen! The problem was, Charlotte would only be a princess till midnight, and the clock was ticking.

"Remember," Tiana heard Prince Naveen tell Charlotte, "you must give Tiana all the money she requires for her restaurant. Because Tiana—she is *my* Evangeline."

Tiana's eyes filled with tears. Prince Naveen really loved her. She hopped toward Naveen just as he was about to kiss Charlotte.

"Wait!" Tiana cried.

"Tiana?" Naveen said.

Charlotte was shocked. "Tiana?" she gasped.

"Don't do this!" Tiana said to Naveen.

"I have to do this!" he answered. "We are running out of time!"

"I won't let you!" Tiana said firmly.

Naveen pleaded with her. "It's the only way to get your dream!"

Tiana watched as Naveen turned back toward Charlotte to kiss her.

"My dream?" Tiana said. "My dream wouldn't be complete without you in it!"

Naveen turned and looked at Tiana. It was getting closer and closer to midnight!

"I love you, Naveen," Tiana said.

"Warts and all?" Naveen asked.

Tiana smiled. "Warts and all."

Naveen took Tiana in his arms.

"All my life, I read about true love in fairy tales," Charlotte said, sniffling, "and now, here it is right in front of me. Tiana, honey, you found it!" She took out a lace hanky, dabbed her eyes, and turned to Prince Naveen. "I'll kiss you, Your Highness," she said breathlessly. No marriage required!"

Tiana and Naveen looked at Charlotte gratefully. Charlotte held the frog to her lips just as the clock chimed twelve. "Oh, my word! Maybe that old clock is a little fast!" she said. Then she kissed him. Nothing happened. She kissed him again, but Naveen was still a frog.

"I'm so sorry," Charlotte said, looking at the frog in her hand.

Naveen and Tiana stared at each other and joined hands. They didn't love being frogs, but they loved each other.

The two frogs suddenly heard Louis calling. He was running toward them with a sorrowful look on his big green face.

"Louis!" Naveen exclaimed. "What is it?"

Louis sadly told them that Facilier had hurt poor Ray. The gator opened his palm. Ray was lying there, his light barely glowing.

Ray opened his eyes. They brightened when he saw Tiana.

"Hey," Ray asked. "How come you're still—?"

"We're staying frogs, Ray," Tiana told him.

"And we're staying together," Naveen said.

Ray smiled. "*Très bien.* I like that very much." Then the little firefly looked up. "Evangeline likes that, too," he said, and his light slowly dimmed.

Tiana, Naveen, and Louis bowed their heads as the rain began to fall. Their tears mixed with the downpour as Ray's light went out.

Chapter 25

A thousand small lights helped lay Ray to rest that night in the bayou. Louis played softly as fireflies from all over came to pay their respects. Tiana and Naveen were there, too, when the clouds parted and starlight sparkled in the sky.

Everyone looked up. There in the sky, the Evening Star, Ray's Evangeline, was shining brightly. And right beside her was a new star no one had ever seen before. A huge grin came over Louis's tear-stained face. Tiana and Naveen held each other close. Ray and his Evangeline were together at last.

Then, under a grand canopy of Spanish moss, all the creatures of the bayou gathered for the wedding of Tiana and her frog prince. The bride wore a lovely leaf on her head as she sat on a lily pad next to her adoring groom. Mama Odie presided over the ceremony with Juju draped around her neck.

"And so, by the power vested in me, I now

pronounce you frog and wife!" Mama Odie said. She leaned toward Prince Naveen. "Get to it!" she said. "Give your lovely bride some sugar!" Mama Odie began to laugh. "Oooh! This is going to be good!"

Prince Naveen kissed Tiana and—*POOF!*—they disappeared in a swirl of sparkling green dust.

When the air cleared, Tiana and Prince Naveen looked at each other in amazement.

Tiana was wearing a shimmering green wedding dress with a crown of flowers in her hair, and Prince Naveen looked dashing in a royal vest and sash. They were both human again!

Mama Odie was still laughing. "Like I told you: Kissing a princess breaks the spell!"

"Once you became my wife," Naveen said, "that made you—"

"A princess!" Tiana exclaimed. "You just kissed yourself a princess!"

"And I'm about to do it again!" Naveen said as the crowd cheered.

The official royal wedding was held in New Orleans's largest cathedral. This time, the guests were all human, including Charlotte, Big Daddy, and the King and Queen of Maldonia.

Eudora watched as her daughter walked down the aisle in the most beautiful wedding gown New Orleans had ever seen.

Princess Tiana and Prince Naveen exited the cathedral through a grand battalion of saluting Maldonian guards. The happy couple stepped into a horse-drawn carriage as Tiana threw her bouquet into the crowd.

Charlotte, of course, caught it.

Princess Tiana purchased the sugar mill the next day. Then, over the next few months, she and Naveen worked hard to transform it into the glamorous restaurant of her dreams.

Tiana perfected every delicious recipe, from the spicy gumbo to the fresh beignets. And if that weren't enough, the restaurant had a stage with a big brass jazz band that featured Louis, the only trumpet-playing alligator in the city.

The night Tiana's restaurant opened, the new princess happily greeted her first guests. Then she approached the table where Eudora was seated with the King and Queen of Maldonia. Eudora was beaming with pride and love. So were Naveen's parents!

"I hope you enjoy the gumbo," Tiana said as she hugged her mother.

"I minced the mushrooms myself!" Prince Naveen said enthusiastically.

Charlotte eagerly took to the dance floor with a young man dressed in full royal finery.

"Who would have thought that the prince would have a younger brother?" she exclaimed. "How old did you say you were?"

"Six and a half," the young prince answered.

Charlotte thought for a moment, and then shrugged her shoulders happily. "Well, I've waited this long!" And she *was* willing to wait a few more years to marry this young prince.

Tiana turned to Prince Naveen and held out her hand to dance. The prince smiled and waltzed her up to the rooftop. A ring of fireflies circled around them. And under the twinkling light of the *two* Evening Stars, Prince Naveen and Princess Tiana danced on top of New Orleans's finest new restaurant, aptly named Tiana's Palace. Tiana's dream of owning a restaurant had finally come true. But now she had even more: She had everything she needed—the love of family and friends. And it had all happened because she had remembered what was important, just as her daddy had said so many years before.